LOOK AND FIND

Disney's Aladdin

Illustrated by Jaime Diaz Studios

Written by Kenny Haas #25

Front cover illustrated by Eddie Young
Lettered by Kelly Hume

Published by
Louis Weber, C.E.O.
Publications International, Ltd.
7373 North Cicero Avenue
Lincolnwood, Illinois 60646

Manufactured in U.S.A.

8 7 6 5 4 3 2 1

ISBN 0-7853-1569-1

HTS BOOKS

AN IMPRINT OF FOREST HOUSE™
School & Library Edition

Millersburg Elementary
Library

Welcome to Agrabah, the home of Aladdin. Do not be fooled by his tattered clothes, for young Aladdin is destined to find a magic lamp. While his future may be bright, right now the Sultan's guards are after him for stealing bread.

Can you find Aladdin and Abu before the guards do? Then locate these other Agrabah residents.

Abu

Aladdin

Princess Jasmine

The Sultan

Rasoul

Jafar

Iago

JUST TURBANS

TRÉS SHEIK

AGRABAH BROILED CHICKEN

SUNDIALS REPAIRED

VASE IS THE PLACE

PYRAMID TIMESHARING

Princess Jasmine's single days are numbered! Being the daughter of the Sultan, she must marry a prince by her birthday, and there are only three days left. Jasmine believes this law is unfair, but many eligible princes have gathered in the palace garden for the chance to win her affection.

Find these princes who don't seem to be Jasmine's type.

Prince
Ima Stinker

Prince
Abracadabra

Prince
Havallama

Prince
Jim Nastic

Prince
Nick Nack

Prince
Chocolotts

I BATHE
HOURLY

In the busy marketplace, Aladdin sees Princess Jasmine and is quite amazed by her beauty. Aladdin rescues Jasmine from an angry apple merchant. As they flee, Aladdin and Jasmine get separated in the crowd.

It will be difficult for Aladdin to find Jasmine with these other Jasmine look-alikes around.

Jasmini

Jasmane

Jasmirelda

Jasmummy

Jasthin

Jasmonkey

Jasmineral

SUNDIALS REPAIRED

GRAND-FATHER SUNDIALS

ALARM CLOCKS

PYRAMID TIME-SHARING

CLEO'S HAREM DANCE STUDIO 6:00 AEROBICS

Delilah's Hair Salon

SAMSON'S GYMNASIUM "DON'T HAVE SAND KICKED IN YOUR FACE!"

FRESH GOAT MILK IT'S NOT BAAAAAAD!

FRESH FISH

TURBANS AND HEADDRESSES

HEADACHE TURBANS

URBAN TURBANS

TEN-GALLON TURBANS

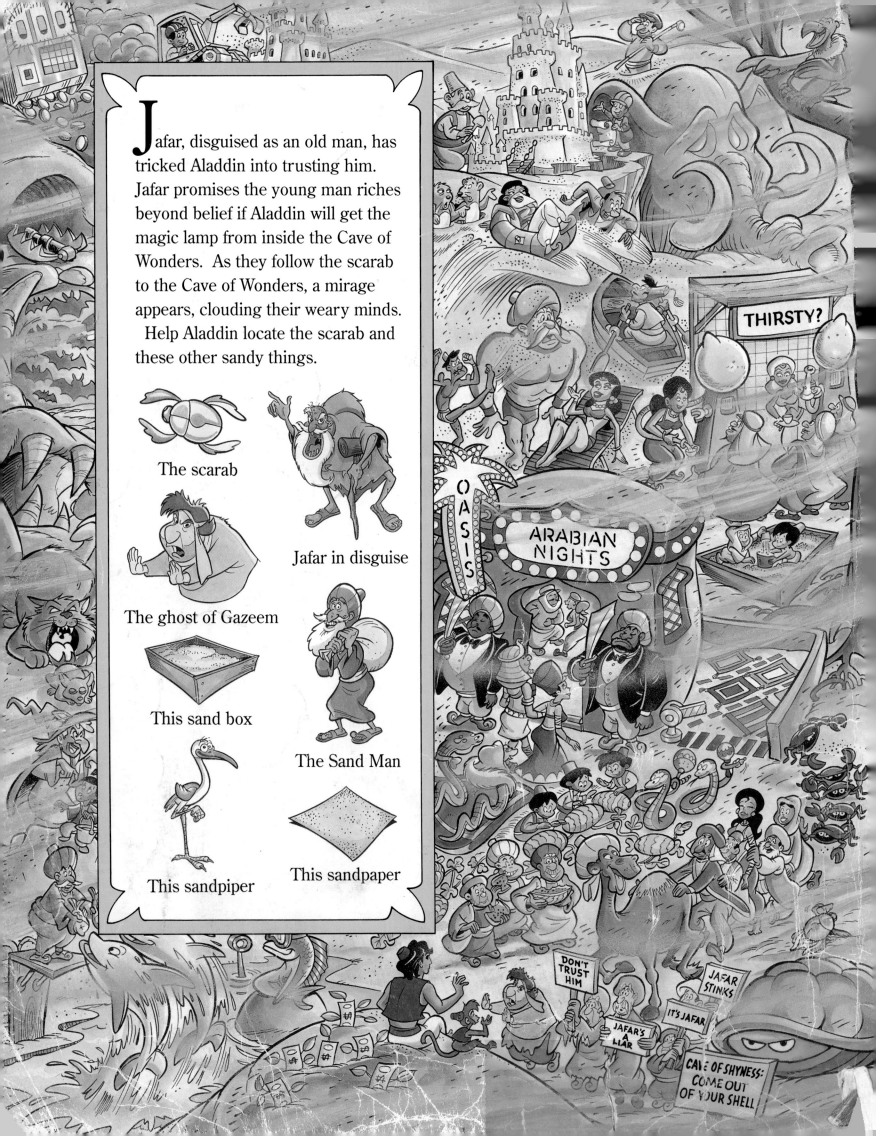

Jafar, disguised as an old man, has tricked Aladdin into trusting him. Jafar promises the young man riches beyond belief if Aladdin will get the magic lamp from inside the Cave of Wonders. As they follow the scarab to the Cave of Wonders, a mirage appears, clouding their weary minds. Help Aladdin locate the scarab and these other sandy things.

The scarab

Jafar in disguise

The ghost of Gazeem

This sand box

The Sand Man

This sandpiper

This sandpaper

The Cave of Wonders contains riches beyond Aladdin's wildest dreams! Temptation is everywhere, but he must touch nothing except the magic lamp!

Help Aladdin keep an eye on Abu and find the lamp and these other treasures.

THE SPHINX FAMILY

Hi Ho Ho Silver

Ruby begonia

Baseball diamond

Diamond in the "ruff-ruff"

Pearly gate

Silver lining

Golden earring

Diamondback rattler

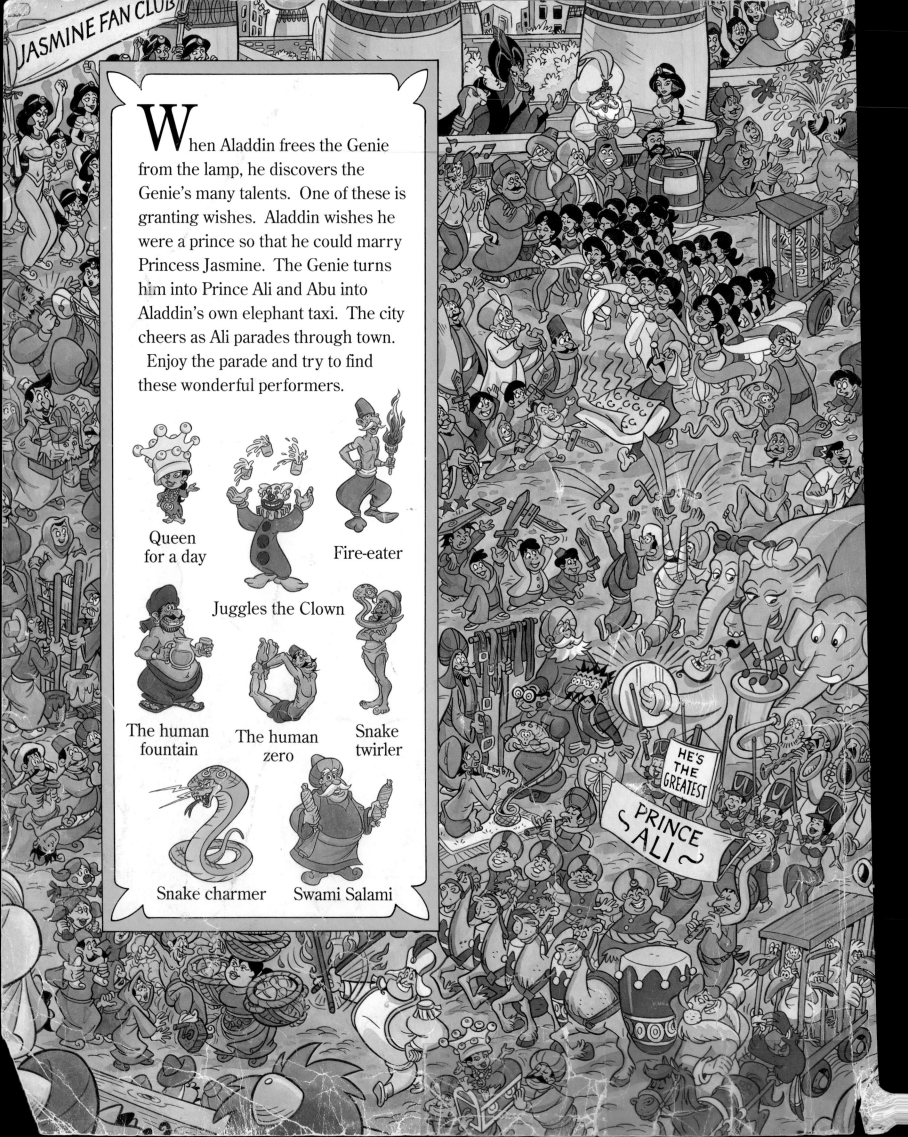

When Aladdin frees the Genie from the lamp, he discovers the Genie's many talents. One of these is granting wishes. Aladdin wishes he were a prince so that he could marry Princess Jasmine. The Genie turns him into Prince Ali and Abu into Aladdin's own elephant taxi. The city cheers as Ali parades through town. Enjoy the parade and try to find these wonderful performers.

Queen for a day

Juggles the Clown

Fire-eater

The human fountain

The human zero

Snake twirler

Snake charmer

Swami Salami

JASMINE FAN CLUB

HE'S THE GREATEST

PRINCE ALI

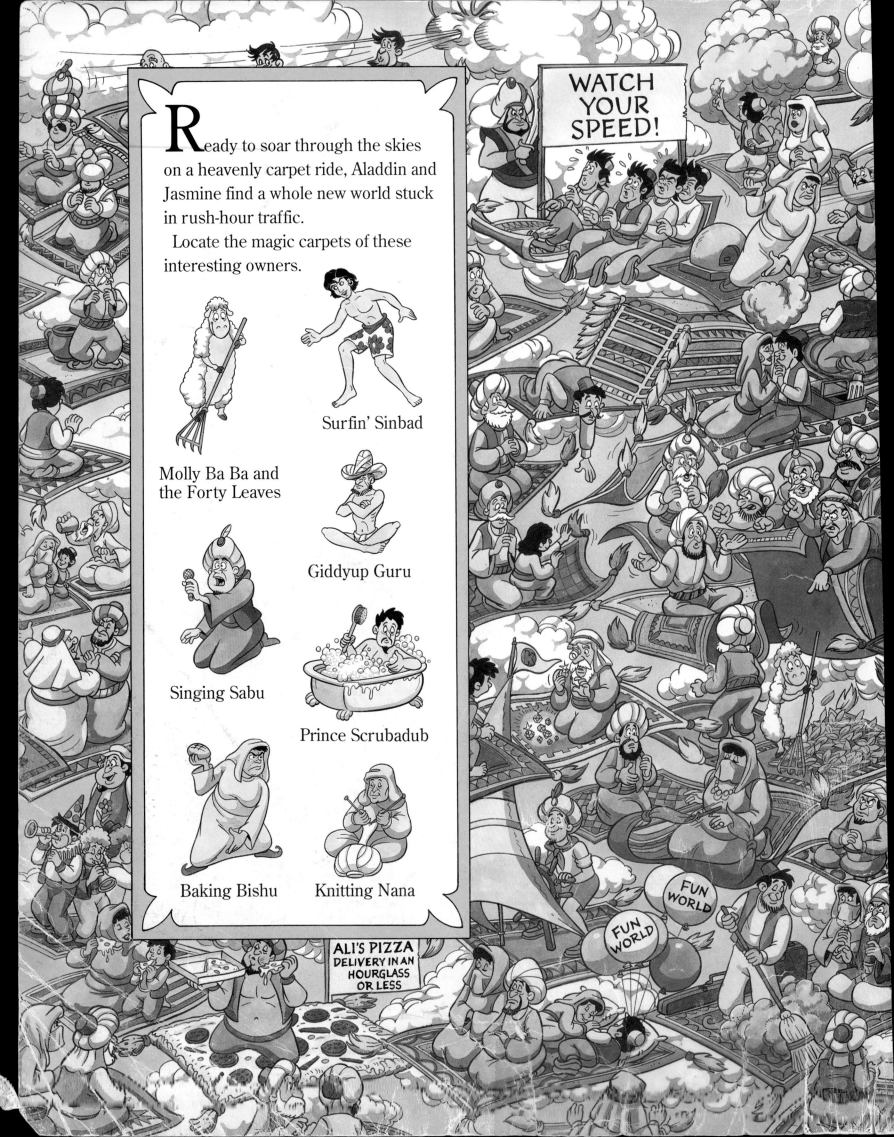

Ready to soar through the skies on a heavenly carpet ride, Aladdin and Jasmine find a whole new world stuck in rush-hour traffic.

Locate the magic carpets of these interesting owners.

Surfin' Sinbad

Molly Ba Ba and the Forty Leaves

Giddyup Guru

Singing Sabu

Prince Scrubadub

Baking Bishu

Knitting Nana

WATCH YOUR SPEED!

ALI'S PIZZA
DELIVERY IN AN
HOURGLASS
OR LESS

FUN WORLD

FUN WORLD

Leaping lamp oil! Iago has stolen Aladdin's lamp, and now Jafar has become the most powerful sorcerer in the universe! Aladdin must find a way to trick Jafar and get back the lamp. It's a good thing Aladdin has plenty of friends, and Jafar has plenty of enemies.

Find the friends who are trying to help Aladdin.

Princess
Jasmine

Royal chef

The
Sultan

Carpet

Loyal subject

Abu

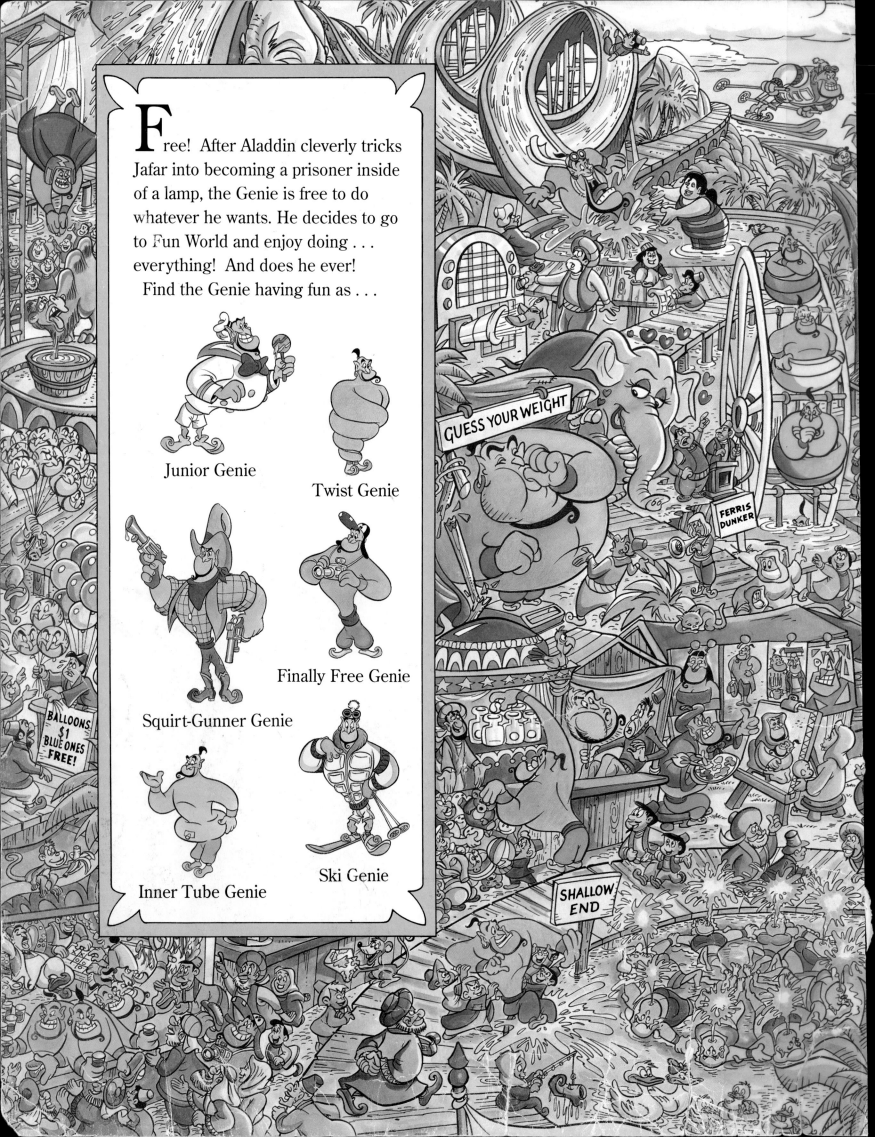

Free! After Aladdin cleverly tricks Jafar into becoming a prisoner inside of a lamp, the Genie is free to do whatever he wants. He decides to go to Fun World and enjoy doing . . . everything! And does he ever!

Find the Genie having fun as . . .

Junior Genie

Twist Genie

Squirt-Gunner Genie

Finally Free Genie

Inner Tube Genie

Ski Genie

BALLOONS $1 BLUE ONES FREE!

GUESS YOUR WEIGHT

FERRIS DUNKER

SHALLOW END

In the palace garden, Jasmine found that the suitors didn't suit her, but she loved their horses. Find these other horse things.

- ☐ Horse scents
- ☐ Horse thief
- ☐ Horse fly
- ☐ Trojan horse
- ☐ Horse hide
- ☐ Horse and buggy

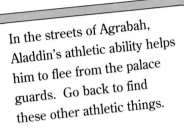

In the streets of Agrabah, Aladdin's athletic ability helps him to flee from the palace guards. Go back to find these other athletic things.

- ☐ Surfboard
- ☐ Golf club
- ☐ Soccer ball
- ☐ Bowling ball
- ☐ Basketball
- ☐ Fishing rod
- ☐ Tennis racket
- ☐ Hockey stick

Aladdin fell in love with Jasmine in the marketplace. Go back and find these other falling things.

- ☐ Someone falling out of a window
- ☐ Someone falling into a well
- ☐ A falling star
- ☐ Someone falling off a camel
- ☐ Someone falling asleep
- ☐ Someone falling into a puddle

Searching the desert for the Cave of Wonders, you find so much sand and so many caves. Go back to spot these caves and other crazy things.

- ☐ Mammoth Cave
- ☐ Cave of Fools
- ☐ Cave of Abu
- ☐ Sand dollars
- ☐ Caveman
- ☐ Sand witch
- ☐ Bat cave
- ☐ Sand crab

In the Cave of Wonders you can look at—BUT DON'T TOUCH!—these treasures.

- ☐ Heart of gold
- ☐ Golden fleece
- ☐ Golden rule
- ☐ Golden retriever
- ☐ "24-carrot" gold
- ☐ Goose that laid the golden egg
- ☐ Goldfish
- ☐ Golden seal

What a parade! The crowd is as much fun to watch as the parade. Go back and find these interesting spectators.

- ☐ Lulu Ladder-Legs
- ☐ Snoozin' Newsman
- ☐ Bunda the Belt Merchant
- ☐ Aesop Coffeetop
- ☐ Rafath the Rock Rider
- ☐ Pickpocket Pratir
- ☐ Hali Hula Hoop

Journey back to the flying carpet traffic jam and find these strange flying carpets.

- ☐ Pizza carpet
- ☐ Dog catcher's carpet
- ☐ Carpet sweeper
- ☐ Taxi carpet
- ☐ Fire carpet
- ☐ Traffic copter carpet
- ☐ Tow carpet

With Jafar taking over the palace, he has attracted some other creepy characters. Go back to the palace and find these other creepy things.

- ☐ Royal rat
- ☐ Raven
- ☐ King snake
- ☐ Mummy
- ☐ A can of worms
- ☐ Knitting spider
- ☐ ABCs of Evil

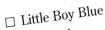

At Fun World there is so much to do, and so much blue! Take a break and spot these other blue things.

- ☐ Little Boy Blue
- ☐ Bluebird
- ☐ Blue suede shoes
- ☐ Royal "blew"
- ☐ Deep blue C
- ☐ Bluebeard
- ☐ Blue cheese